R.N. CHEVALIER
ILLUSTRATED BY JASMINE CHEVALIER

JAY AND ROWAN

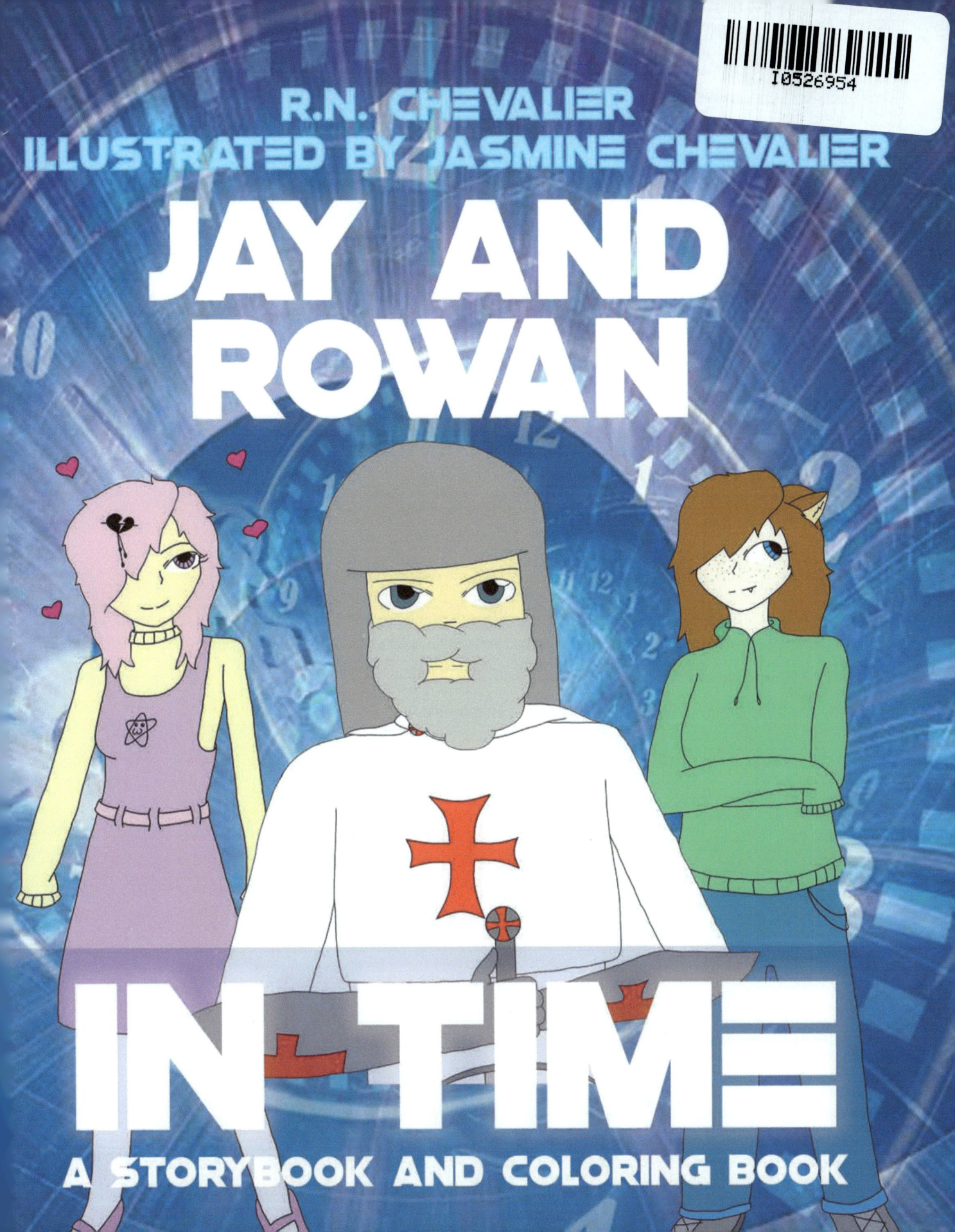

IN TIME

A STORYBOOK AND COLORING BOOK

Visit our website at www.StillwaterPress.com for more information.

First Stillwater River Publications Edition

Library of Congress Control Number 2019933284

ISBN-13: 978-1-950-33903-7
ISBN-10: 1-950-33903-3

1 2 3 4 5 6 7 8 9 10

Written by R.N. Chevalier
Illustrations by Jasmine "Jay" Chevalier
Cover design by Kody Lavature

Published by Stillwater River Publications, Pawtucket, RI, USA.

DEDICATION

To Donna Chevalier, who is my motivation for everything.

To Jasmine "Jay" Chevalier, Thank you for all your hard work.

IN MEMORIAM

My grandparents:

Mozart Goulet

5 May 1905 – 12 June 1998

Aline Soucy Goulet

17 December 1914 – 27 February 1987

Doris Chevalier Denis Englehart

13 June 1917 – 3 March 1975

When I needed to name the knight that the girls would be befriended by I needed someone who was familiar yet whose name would fit. Enter my grandfather, Mozart Goulet. Things he did as a young man made him the perfect person to be the knight.

CHAPTER 1

Bang! Bang! Bang! echoes through the dark house.

"Rowan, wake up!" Jay quietly shouts. "Get up!" She pounds gently on the door three more times.

"Rowan, open the door!" She bangs again without a pause.

"Come on, Rowan! Open th…"

The door opens to reveal the red-eye, shaggy haired teenager.

"Shh!" She whispers loudly. "My parents are still asleep." She rubs the sleep from her eyes.

"It's five-thirty in the morning. What are you doing here?"

"My dad came home a couple of hours ago," Jay explains. "He was all beat up. As mom and I were bringing dad to the hospital, he said his invention works!"

"What invention?" Rowan asks with a yawn. "You mean that crazy time machine?"

"Yes," Jay confirms excitedly. "That crazy time machine. He said that he and his friend, Pete, went back in time and were in a battle with the Knights Templar."

"Wow," Rowan interrupts nonchalantly, this time a bit more awake. "I am related to a Templar. No one important, mind you, at least I don't think he was important, but a Templar nonetheless."

"Rowan!" Jay interrupts her now. "I'm not done. Before my dad passed out, he told me where the time machine is and that his friend is still lost in the past."

"You're serious, aren't you?" Rowan asks confused.

"Yes, I'm serious! Do you think I'd be here at five-thirty if I wasn't?"

Jay takes a deep breath. "While we were at the hospital, a police officer overheard Dad tell me what happened and now, when he's done at the hospital, my dad is going to be arrested for what happened to Pete."

"And the cop believed him?"

"Not about the time traveling, but the officer thinks my dad was drinking or doing drugs and hurt Pete."

"So, what are *we* gonna do?" Rowan asks.

"*We're* gonna find my dad's time machine, go back in time and rescue my dad's friend."

"Okay." Rowan says as she gets dressed. "Let's do this." The two teens quietly leave the house. They get into Jay's father's car and head to the highway.

"What do you know about your ancestor?" Jay asks Rowan. "And what do you know about where we're going?"

"Not a lot," Rowan begins as she reclines her seat back a bit. "His name was Mozart de Goulet. He was a scribe and a warrior. He served with Jacques de Molay,

the leader of the Templars, when the members were arrested. All I know is that when the Templars fell, he escaped with a small group to the Americas. He married a native girl soon after he got here and, eventually, here I was."

"Who were they fighting in the end?" Jay asks.

"King Philip IV of France," Rowan continues. "Most of them were arrested on October 13, 1307. That was a Friday. That's why Friday the 13th is considered unlucky. De Moley discovered the plot and while most of the Templars were being arrested several ships escaped, two while de Goulet and several artifacts were being chased. He made it to the ships after they had undocked from the pier."

As Rowan finishes her story, Jay pulls off the road and continues several blocks to an old, abandoned gas station. She pulls around back and shuts the car off. They get out of the car and walk around to the side of the building.

There they discover a broken window. As they approach the window, the snapping of broken glass breaks the silence.

"The window was broken from the inside," Jay whispers to Rowan as they approach the building.

They carefully enter through the broken window, landing on a desk first then the floor. They slowly make their way through the darkness. It takes a few minutes for their eyes to adjust to the lightless room.

They exit the office and make their way into the repair bay. There they find a steel storage container the size of a small bus.

"The time machine must be inside this storage container," Jay says as she unlatches the heavy door. Rowan lends a hand.

When the doors swing open, the two see that the steel container **is** the time machine. There are huge wire coils in all four corners. Against one of the long walls are electrical generators on shelves that rise from the floor to the ceiling.

Against the short wall opposite the doors are more shelves of electrical generators. Against the other long wall are computer servers. In the middle of the row of servers is a single monitor and keyboard. There are two chairs in front of the keyboard.

Jay sits in the chair behind the keyboard and monitor while Rowan sits in the other seat. Jay starts the computer and a low hum comes from the servers connected to the monitor.

The monitor begins to glow to life as data starts streaming across its face. It takes nearly five minutes for the systems to boot up. Finally, the data stops scrolling and the information on the screen changes.

"Oh wow," Jay says in disbelief.

"What is it?" Rowan asks nervously.

"According to these logs," Jay continues, "when my dad activated the machine, they ended up in France on the night of October 12, 1307."

"That's when they must have come up against the Templars," Rowan suggests.

"I think you're right," Jay agrees. "And that's where Dad's friend, Pete, is."

CHAPTER 2

Jay takes the time to become familiar with the software, and with Rowan's help, is ready to activate the machine. The screen shows that all systems are ready to go.

"Are you ready, Rowan?" Jay asks.

"Ready as I'll ever be," Rowan replies.

"I hope I got these controls right," Jay says as she keys in the activation commands.

"What?" Rowan says with wide-eyed nervousness as Jay starts to giggle.

Jay hits the *enter* button and the four coils start to glow with a slow pulse. The pulses become quicker and quicker as the seconds tick by.

As the pulses quicken, the air in the container begins to shimmer with silvery-gray sparkles. In fifteen seconds, the coils are glowing steadily as red and green sparkles join the silvery-gray ones.

Ten seconds after that, the coils' glows fade away and the glistening sparkles dim away to nothingness.

"Is that it?" Rowan asks sarcastically. "A light show?"

"Oh boy," Jay says with concern.

"What's wrong?"

"The computer says that we're in India and it's 6,700 BC." Jay tells her.

"I thought we were going to 1307 France?"

"I must have goofed somewhere," Jay replies.

"What!" Rowan shouts with fear causing her voice to squeal.

"I'll figure it out," Jay replies confidently. She breaks out her father's notebook from under the keyboard and begins studying its contents.

"Give me about twenty, maybe thirty minutes," Jay says.

"Well then, I'm going outside to look around."

"Be careful and stay close," Jay responds.

"That's the plan," Rowan reassures her as she heads toward the steel doors.

"I'll join you when I solve the problem," Jay answers.

After a few seconds, Rowan opens the door and is immediately blinded by the midday sun.

"Wow!" Rowan shouts with surprise.

"What's wrong?" Jay shouts back with a jolt.

"It's daytime," Rowan answers. "And the sun is really bright."

"What?" Jay asks with surprise as she gets up and heads toward the door.

The two step outside to find the sun sitting high in the sky. The air is dry and the wind is hot.

The sounds of explosions, like fireworks only louder, catch their attention. It's coming from over the hill about a hundred yards away. The hill is only about sixty feet tall, so it only takes a few minutes for them to run to the top.

What they see from the top of the hill leaves both of them unable to speak for several minutes. Hanging in the distant sky are two enormous spaceships, several miles around, shooting missiles at each other.

In the twenty-mile space between the two spaceships are hundreds of tiny, one man vessels, buzzing around like flies, trying to destroy each other.

"What the…?" She cuts herself off.

"Jay!" Rowan cries out. "Do you know what's going on?"

"Not a clue," Jay answers. "But it's so cool!"

"Well I do," Rowan says. "At least I think I know what's going on."

"Tell me," Jay demands.

"Well, one of those ships must be Krishna and the other is Lord Saulva. The village under them must be the city of Dwarka. See the right side of the village? See how it looks metallic and the rest of it looks like mud brick?

"Yeah," Jay answers. "So what?"

"So, that's the part of the city that sinks into the sea when Krishna dies. But it doesn't sink, it flies away."

"What are you saying? That those are *aliens* on the ground?"

"Exactly," Rowan says. "Aliens living with humans."

"How do you know so much about this stuff?" Jay asks.

"*Ancient Aliens*," she replies.

"What, the TV show?"

"Yep. My father watches it every day."

"I thought that was all fake."

"Look over there!" Rowan points to the two massive spaceships battling in the distance. "Does that *look* like it's fake?"

"It'll take about two hours for the generators to fully charge," Jay tells Rowan. "Give me ten more minutes and then we'll make our way closer to the city."

Rowan agrees and the two carefully make their way toward the city when Jay finishes reprogramming the computer. It takes about forty-five minutes for them to reach the buildings on the outskirts of the city.

They make their way between the houses, heading for the center of city. They pass a rope between two buildings with robes hanging from them.

"Look," Jay says. "Laundry." She touches one of the robes. "It's nearly dry," She continues as she takes it off the line and tosses it to Rowan.

"What are you doing?" Rowan asks with surprise.

"We're only going to borrow them," Jay explains. "We need to fit in. We'll bring them back on our way back to the time machine."

"Okay, then." Rowan says. They put the robes on and continue their trek, wary of their surroundings.

It takes them ten minutes to get to a crowd of people. Just beyond the crowd is a man. As Jay and Rowan make their way through the forest of people, the man becomes more visible.

Rowan freezes in awe when the man turns around.

"What is it?" Jay asks.

"Look," Is Rowan's reply.

The man at the head of the crowd is over eight feet tall… and blue skinned! And, in the center of his forehead, is a third eye!

"Is that Krishna?" Jay asks.

"No," Rowan says with a stunned tone. "That's Shiva, Shiva the Destroyer."

"Who's he?"

"He's a god,"

"No, really, who is he?"

"He's an alien mistaken to be a god."

"It's alright now, my friends." Shiva tells the crowd of people now that the smaller ships have cleared the skies. "Our enemies have been repelled for now. It is safe again."

Two of Shiva's guards approach him, whispering in his ear. Before the guard can finish his message, a whirlwind appears in the center of the plaza twenty yards away.

The whirlwind forms into a concentrated spherical vortex of thick gray clouds, spitting short lightning bolts from its center. The ball shrinks to about twenty feet across before it stabilizes as the roar of thundering wind becomes deafening.

Without warning, the sphere explodes with a force powerful enough to knock those standing closest to it to the ground. When the smoke clears, in place of the sphere is a metal device, looking like a cross between an acorn and a bell, standing fifteen feet tall and nearly ten feet wide.

The crowd, except Shiva, his guards, Jay, and Rowan, gasp loudly and fall to their knees when a door on the side of device opens.

Out of the opening come three men. The two on the ends are wearing strange black uniforms. The man in the middle is wearing a gray uniform. He has black hair, parted far to the right and a mustache that grew only under his nose.

"Mein, Fuhrer," The man on the right starts. *"Die glocke… Es klappt!"*

"What did he say?" Rowan asks.

"That's German," Jay says. "He said, 'My leader… the bell… it works."

"Oh my god!" Rowan says in a stunned stutter. That's… that's Hitler! Adolph Hitler!"

"You mean Nazi Germany's Adolph Hitler?"

"Yes!"

"How can he be here?"

"That's the bell," Rowan explains. "One of the Nazi's Wonder Weapons. Researchers speculated that it might have been a time machine. Most of the blueprints were discovered when Germany fell but the prototype was never found."

"Now we know why. But Hitler killed himself in the bunker."

"There was also a rumor that Hitler had as many as seven doubles in case anyone tried to assassinate him. His body was never truly identified. It must have been one of his doubles who died in the bunker."

"*Sie sind alle Gefangene des Dritten Reiches,*" Hitler shouts at the kneeling crowd.

"What did he say"?

"You are all prisoners of the Third Reich," Jay repeats as the men on both sides of Hitler draw their rifles.

"This is bad," Rowan says as the man on the left points at Shiva and pulls the trigger. The bullet hits Shiva in the chest with no affect.

"Destroy them," Shiva says without emotion. The two guards draw their weapons and fire. They take out the men on the ends then, before he can draw his own pistol, the guards shoot Hitler. They fire several shots into the device, destroying the electronics inside. The crowd cheers and turn their devotion back to Shiva.

"Well," Jay says softly. "Now we know what really happened to Adolph Hitler."

"Let's get back to the time machine," Rowan suggests.

"Let's go." The two make their way through the crowd.

They get several yards beyond the last of the people when the alarm on Rowan's cellphone starts to ring loudly. Rowan removes her robe to shut it off and the people see the strange clothes under the stolen garments.

"Capture them," Shiva commands coldly. The crowd focuses on Jay and Rowan. Jay takes her robe off and the two begin to run as fast as they can with half of the population of the city chasing them.

They weave around the small houses, through the narrow streets and tiny alleyways, trying to evade the city dwellers. The teens come across the rope that held the robes they borrowed when they entered the city.

"I think we lost them," Jay says when they stop to catch their breaths.

"I think you're right," Rowan replies. Just then a crowd of people turn a corner two buildings away.

"Then again," Rowan continues, "I don't think you're right."

Twenty minutes later the two enter the time machine. Rowan locks the door as Jay powers up the coils. The pounding on the huge steel doors startles them both.

"Ten seconds," Jay reads from the screen as the banging continues. The coils glow and air glistens.

The banging stops.

CHAPTER 3

"**W**here are we?" Rowan asks when the loud humming and light show subsides.

"We're in France," Jay answers.

"Cool," Rowan replies. "Now, *when* are we?"

"October 12, 1307… a few hours before Dad and Pete get here."

"Then, how can they get here if we have the time machine?"

"Outside it's yesterday morning, so right now they're getting ready to leave."

"But we got here before they did… before they will get here?"

"Exactly," Jay smiles back.

"This is all too confusing," Rowan confesses. "I know we're actually doing it but it's still confusing."

"Not really." Jay replies as she takes the lace from one of her sneakers.

"Think of time as a piece of string…" Jay holds the lace from tip to tip and makes it taunt. She slides her left fingers up several inches.

"This is the past." She moves her right fingers about six inches from her left fingers.

"This is the present. Time can be 'looped' so the present meets the past or the future." She brings her fingers together forming a loop with the lace.

"Now I get it," Rowan affirms.

"But if we are not very, very careful, we can mess things up so bad we could wipe out history." She slides her fingers quickly, tightening the lace as it drops it to the floor.

"Well then, we'll have to be really careful."

"I agree." Jay puts the lace back on her sneaker. "Are you ready to see what it's like outside? We have about six hours until Dad and Pete get here."

The two open the doors and wince against the late afternoon sunlight. They find themselves in a small clearing surrounded by thick woods. They find a narrow path behind the time machine.

The duo makes their way through the overgrown brush.

After about thirty minutes, they come upon a dirt road through the thick woods.

"Let's mark this path so we can find the time machine later," Rowan suggests, and Jay agrees. They gather stones and lay them in a line of five with the smallest stone closest to the shrubs and largest stone closest to the road like an arrow pointing the way.

"That'll do it," Jay says.

"I'm going to take a picture too," Rowan says as she takes out her cellphone and takes a photo of the entrance.

"Good idea," Jay says as the two choose a direction and start walking.

Thirty minutes pass when Jay and Rowan come across a few blueberry bushes.

"Alright!" Jay says with a smile. "I'm so hungry." She grabs a bush of berries and starts eating.

"Me too," Rowan states as she grabs a handful of berries and stuffs them in her mouth.

The two girls finish the last of the berries off the branches they are holding. Having eaten their fill, they start walking again.

Within minutes they cross a small brook. They drop to their knees at the edge of the brook and start drinking. When they finish drinking, they sit for a few minutes to let their meal settle in their bellies.

They start walking again after about ten minutes. As they approach a sharp bend in the road, they hear an unfamiliar clanking noise – like two empty halves of a coconut being banged together.

Jay and Rowan stop as the noise gets louder. Both girls stand frozen with their mouths hanging wide open when the noise comes around the bend.

There in front of them is a man on a huge horse. The mysterious man is dressed in a white, long sleeve top that goes down nearly to his knees. On his chest is a red cross with the four ends split, making it an eight-sided cross. He is wearing a chainmail headpiece, exposing only his beard covered face. His pants are also white, being made of the same material as his top. His metal boot covered feet are secured in the stirrups of his saddle. A huge, intricately decorated sword hangs from the black leather belt around his waist. A flowing white cape finishes his outfit.

This man is sitting on a brown stallion with shining black eyes. The beast stands nearly six feet at its front shoulders. A red blanket shows between the horse and the metal studded leather saddle. Its head and face are protected by metal armor.

When the horse spies the two girls, it stops dead in its tracks, kicking up and flailing its front legs in response to the threat.

The two girls step back from the stallion's reaction and fall flat on their backsides. The man on the horse starts laughing as Jay and Rowan pick themselves up from the ground.

"Who might you be, strangers?" The man asks in a burly voice of English with a very heavy French accent. "Your faces are not known to me, nor are your garments."

The two girls are too stunned to speak. "Don't you naves know how to speak? He asks with irritation in his voice. "Are you both dumb?"

"No, we're not dumb," Jay replies with irritation of her own. "You took us by surprise, that's all."

"Never mind the fact you nearly killed us," Rowan grumbles at him.

"My apologies, lass," The man continues. "I am Mozart De Goulet of the Order of the Knights Templar. Good day to you both."

"I'm Jay and this is my friend Rowan," The teenager replies, now more relaxed.

"What land are ye from to speak so oddly… and dress even stranger?" He asks with an odd expression.

"We are from the United States. A place called Rhode Island." Jay tells him. Mozart De Goulet looks at the two teens with a look of bewilderment.

"It's one of the New England states," Rowan tries to clarify.

"I was not aware of England having colonies elsewhere," De Goulet says with confusion.

"The colony was kept a secret because no one knew if we would survive." Jay takes a breath and continues. "We have a warning for Jacques De Moley. It's about the treason of King Philip of France."

"We are aware of the treachery of Philip," De Goulet tells them. "Our plan is already in play."

"We may be able to help," Jay tells De Goulet. "We have information that De Moley will find invaluable."

"Well… that's a different story," De Goulet says as a smile returns to his face. "Why didn't you say so?"

"We tried," Jay answered with a more relaxed tone.

"Good thinking," Rowan whispers in Jay's ear.

"Thanks," Jay replies. "Now you better know a few things that they don't know so they don't kill us."

"Gee thanks," Rowan replies flatly.

"Join me as a guest of the Templar Order. Follow me and tonight we will feast and hear of your stories." Mozart slowly guides his horse between the girls and the two follow him down the path.

Rowan takes out her cellphone and takes several quick photos of De Goulet.

Hours have passed since Jay and Rowan started following Mozart De Goulet. The forest abruptly ends at the edge of a vast pasture with rolling hills like swells in an ocean of green.

The sun now sits just above the treeline, casting long, dark shadows across the landscape. On the edge of a rise about two miles away the outline of a castle appears as a dark yet tiny silhouette.

"There is our destination, *mes amies*," De Goulet tells them. "Our stronghold of Metz." As they continue their journey, the castle-like structure starts looking more like a cathedral. When they reach the last rise, they can make out smaller buildings around the cathedral fanning out in all directions.

"Wow," Jay muses. "That looks like a small city."

"Oui," De Goulet answers. "The city of Metz, France. The Mosselle and Seille rivers run on the far sides of the city and over that ridge." De Goulet points to the distant right. "That is the land of Germania." The girls' gazes follow his hand and they nod in understanding.

The three continue their trek toward the city. They travel another three miles before they reach the outer buildings. Darkness has enveloped most of the sky with a sliver of daylight still visible on the distant horizon.

A faint *whooshing* sound suddenly becomes audible. The stallion bucks nervously. The sound fades away after a few seconds as does a faint glow over a nearby rise. De Goulet doesn't notice the glow, but Jay and Rowan do.

"I'm pretty sure that's my dad and Pete," Jay whispers to Rowan, who nods in agreement. They make their way through the maze of closely built houses.

They get to the end of a row of houses and the street opens to a large plaza. At the far end of the plaza is the cathedral. They make their way around the massive structure, and on the far side is a modest structure.

"This is our chapel," De Goulet informs the teens. "We must pray here before we go into the cathedral." They go inside the small chapel and sit in the small wooden pews, praying for around fifteen minutes.

They stand and exit the chapel through a door on the wall on the far side of the room. Rowan takes a few photos of the chapel.

The door leads to a twenty-foot-long corridor ending with two doors. Each door is nine and a half feet tall by four feet wide, arched at their tops. Both doors are full murals made of brightly colored stained glass.

The door on the right depicts the crucifixion of Jesus of Nazareth and the door on the left depicts his resurrection. The brilliance of the colored glass is visible even in the dull candlelight emanating from inside the huge cathedral.

Along the right wall is an eight-foot-wide opening. Five feet in, the floor becomes a staircase. De Goulet takes a torch from its holder on the wall and lights it. He hands a torch to Rowan They stand still for a few seconds while they let their eyes adjust to the light which extends in a six-foot radius around the torch.

They spend a full five minutes walking down. Jay counts two hundred and fifty steps from top to bottom. At the bottom is a seven-foot-tall by four foot wide door made of timbers about nine inches square and held together by five iron bands.

The creaking of the door breaks the silence. As the door swings open the three can hear the distant sounds of people. They pass through the door and close it behind them.

De Goulet leads Jay and Rowan down the dark corridor. As they continue, a dim light becomes visible in the distance it only takes a few seconds before the dull sounds become distinct voices of people mingling with the sound of sharply played happy music.

Another fifteen seconds finds the three at a right turn. The light shines brightly at the end of a short corridor. They walk down and enter a hall that is two hundred feet long and forty feet wide.

There are four long wooden tables in the hall lined on both sides with chairs. There is a large gap between the middle tables. In that gap is a smaller table that has three larger chairs on the far side.

There are about four hundred people squeezed in the hall. The echoing chatter is like white noise to the teens.

There is a second-floor balcony all around the hall. A four-man band is on the far end and there are sporadic groups of people around the whole balcony.

Everyone is eating and drinking. As the people see Jay and Rowan, they become silent. All eyes fall on the teens as they approach the middle table.

"Ah, Mozart!" The man in the big center chair shouts happily with a huge smile when he sees De Goulet emerge from a group of people in front of him.

His smile is short lived when, from behind the same group, emerge Jay and Rowan.

"Worry not, my liege." De Goulet tells the man. "These young ones are from a new England colony. They know of King Philip's treachery and have information you will find valuable. They are in need of food and rest while they wait for their companions."

"Are you Jacques De Moley?" Rowan asks sheepishly as she steps out from behind De Goulet.

"I surely am, young wench." De Moley answers sharply.

"My name is Rowan, sir." She answers softly.

"Speak up, girl!" De Moley snaps loudly.

"My name is Rowan, sir!" She shouts back more afraid than courageous. De Moley starts laughing boisterously, allowing Jay and Rowan to relax slightly.

"You have news for me?"

"Yes, sir, I do."

"Then out with it."

"By dawn you and your knights will be arrested by King Philip's soldiers."

"How do you know this to be, girl?" His anger coming through in his tone.

"I can't tell you," Rowan replies in a voice riddled with anxiety.

"In God's name, why not!" His screaming brings the room to total silence.

"What she means, my liege," Jay steps in loudly, "is that she doesn't know. Several days ago, we were lost in the woods when we came across a small group of French soldiers. We overheard them discussing the raids then decided we had to find you and warn you."

"We know of Philip's plans," De Moley admits to the teens, "only not the time." He turns to De Goulet. "Our time is short. Get the arc and the grail to the ships. Put one on each. You must accompany the grail on its journey."

"I understand my liege." De Goulet acknowledges. "I will not fail. We will not fail." The two men grip each other's wrists in an ancient handshake. Both girls stand stunned.

"You possess both the arc of the covenant *and* the holy grail?" Rowan asks.

"Amongst other items, yes," De Moley tells them. "And now they must leave this land."

"Can we see them?" Jay asks.

"If you wish, you can ride with De Goulet to escort them to the port of La Rochelle." De Moley replies. The three turn and walk quickly toward the exit. As they walk, De Goulet points to various men sitting along the long table. These men get up and start walking behind the trio.

When the group, now numbering ten, gets outside, darkness greets them. They walk together toward the stables when a disturbance in the brush to the left of the building draws their attention.

"You, in the brush!" De Goulet shouts as the eight knights draw their swords. "Who goes there?"

"Wait!" A voice comes from the brush. "We come in peace." Out of the brush come two men who step out into the moonlight.

"Dad!" Jay says with emotion in her voice as she runs to him. She gives him a long, tight hug.

"Jay," He replies with stunned confusion. "How? When? I don't understand."

"When you go home you tell me and mom a little of what happened and where your time machine was. Rowan and I came here to help you and Pete."

"What about me?" Pete asks with dread.

"Dad said you guys fought with the Templars and that you were left in the past. We came to warn you."

"Thanks," Jay's dad says. "Now that we know it works, let's go home before we contaminate the timeline any worse. Do you remember where your, I mean my, time machine is?"

"Yes, but it'll take us about three hours to get to it." Jay tells him.

"I can saddle a horse for you and Rowan to share," De Goulet offers. "You can make it there in an hour."

"That's how long it will take Pete and me to get back on foot."

"Then it is settled." De Goulet says as he turns his focus on the man standing by the last stall.

"Cologne, saddle that horse for our young friends." The man nods and starts his task.

"Thank you for your help, masseur De Goulet," Jay says as she gives the big man a hug.

"Yeah," Rowan adds. "Thanks." She also gives him a hug. A few minutes pass quietly before Cologne walks over.

"The horse is ready," He reports.

"I will ride with you," De Goulet volunteers.

"No," Rowan pleads. "You must make it to the ships and save the artifacts." Jay and Rowan mount the horse with De Goulet's assistance.

"Jay, I'll meet you at home as soon as we get back. Wait for me there. I love you, kiddo." A father kisses his daughter's cheek as she bends over low to reach him.

"Love you," Jay replies as the horse slowly trots away. "I'll see you at home."

A loud disturbance at the far end of the cathedral catches everyone's attention. From around the corner of the massive building come King Philip's troops, numbering around sixty.

"Get going!" De Goulet shouts from his horse as he draws his sword. "We will fight them off while you make your escape." He turns his attention to his men, and the coming horde.

"Attack!" De Goulet shouts and the small band of Templars charge the advancing soldiers. From the chapel entrance emerge a stream of Templar Knights from the great hall, obviously alerted at the moment the king's men came into view.

Jay and Rowan race away along the road they arrived on while Dad and Pete run in the opposite direction. Jay and Rowan turn to look at the cathedral as the horse gallops over the nearest rise.

The last thing they see is a second wave of Philip's soldiers approaching from across the courtyard.

CHAPTER 4

Rowan opens the steel doors of the time machine after the lights in the coils dim to black. The doors swing open and the two see the familiar interior of the abandoned garage. They quickly exit the building the same way they went in.

They get to the car and as Jay unlocks the door Rowan rests on the hood of the car.

"Wow," Rowan whispers sounding surprised. "Hmm, that's odd. The engine is still warm." Jay gets the door open.

"Get in," she tells Rowan. "Let's get out of here." They get in the car and drive away.

"Look at the clock." Rowan says with a stunned tone. "We've been gone for less than fifteen minutes."

"And hopefully everything out there is fixed." Jay says, motioning to the world outside of the car.

The car arrives at Jay's house twenty minutes later. The two enter to find Jay's mother sitting at the kitchen table, anger shinning brightly on her face.

"Where have you been, young lady?" Her mother asks angrily. "And who is this?" She points to Rowan and before Jay can respond she continues, "This is a family matter so I would appreciate it if you would go to wherever it is you live and let me deal with my daughter."

Rowan looks at Jay with tear filled eyes and leaves the house too stunned to speak. She opens the door to leave but Jay's father is blocking the way. She brushes past him and runs down the street.

"Who was your friend, Jay?" Dad asks.

"That was Rowan, Dad." Jay explains. "She's been my friend for, like, forever." Dad shrugs as mom raises her voice.

"Hey," Mom shouts at the two. "I'm still here! Where have you two been?"

Jay and her dad spend the next hour telling Mom about their adventures in the past. Now that they're finished, Jay goes to her room to lie down. Within minutes there is a slight knocking on Jay's bedroom window.

Jay opens the blinds to find Rowan on the outside, crying uncontrollably. Jay opens the window and Rowan slowly makes her way into the house.

"What's wrong, Rowan?"

"I got home and went to my room and my room wasn't there." Jay looks confused as Rowan continues. "My parents came out of their room and freaked out. I freaked out. My father wasn't my father, he was some other guy. They said they didn't know me. They said they would call the police. What's going on?" She continues crying.

"We'll figure it out, Rowan. I promise." Jay replies as she consoles her friend.

After a few minutes Jay stiffens up and looks around the room. She gets up and goes to her tablet without saying a word. She logs on and searches *Knights Templar*. She immerses herself into the information on the screen for several minutes.

"I know what happened," Jay shouts with excitement. It's right here." She points to the screen.

"What is?" Rowan asks, still sobbing. "What did you find?"

"On October 13, 1307," Jay reads from the screen. "Jacques De Moley and his second-in-command, Mozart De Goulet, were arrested at the cathedral in Metz, France and imprisoned."

"So my ancestor was arrested with the others and never made it to the new world and I was never born." Rowan's eyes grow wide as she continues, "The only way to fix this is to go back to France and make sure De Goulet gets on that ship. I don't want to go back there. We came this close to getting killed." She puts her thumb and forefinger about an eighth of an inch apart.

The two teens sit on Jay's beddeep in thought. Thirty minutes go by and Rowan starts to sob again.

"What's wrong, Rowan?" Jay asks expressing sincere sympathy.

"I can't think of any other way to fix this." Rowan's voice is quivering with fear.

"Neither can I but I'll be right there with you. We'll fix this, we just have to stay strong and sharp." Rowan stiffens up and stops sobbing. She wipes her tears away and forces a smile.

"I'll get some supplies and we'll get out of here," Jay says as she gets up and exits the room.

Jay comes back after ten minutes with a small backpack with snacks, several flashlights, a lighter, and a few other items.

"My mom took the car so we'll have to walk to the garage."

"Where's your dad?"

"Asleep. You ready?"

"Yeah, let's do this."

The girls get up and quietly exit the house. It takes several hours for them to get to the time machine on foot. They enter through the broken window and make their way to the storage container.

Jay activates the machine and after the familiar light show Rowan opens the door. They are greeted by the blackness of night.

"What time is it?" Rowan asks.

"It is 9:30 pm," Jay answers. "We are just getting to the cathedral." They step outside and lock the doors. "It will be two hours before the generators are recharged and an hour and a half before King Philip's soldiers arrest De Moley and De Goulet."

"We've got to get to the cathedral quick and warn everyone before it's too late," Jay says as she starts running slowly toward their destiny. Rowan follows behind and catches up quickly. It takes them an hour and a quarter to get to the cathedral.

The girls arrive at the back of the stables just as the group, including the past them, emerges from the chapel. Jay and Rowan hide behind a cart of hay as the group walk over to get horses.

Cologne comes over and begins to saddle the horse for Jay and Rowan as the two girls make their way around the building in the shadows. De Goulet walks away from the group and both Jay and Rowan make their way through the dark to get closer to him.

"Masseur De Goulet," Jay whispers to him. "Masseur De Goulet, it's me, Jay."

"Jay?" He asks shockingly. "But how can this be? I just left you standing with your father. How can you be here?"

"That's very hard to explain right now," Jay says. "You must listen to me. King Phillip's men are going to attack any minute and capture you. You have to escape and make it to the ships."

"But if the king's men are going to attack, I must fight."

"You can't." Rowan cuts in. "We can't tell you why, but you must escape. Please trust us." Tears start flowing from Rowan's eyes.

"But I must fight, *mes amies*," De Goulet says sorrowfully. "It is the Templar code. I must."

"Attack!" Echoes through the quiet just as de Goulet finishes his sentence. Rustling from the surrounding woods follows immediately.

De Goulet turns and the three, along with the group standing in the open, see King Phillip's soldiers emerge from the woods.

"Get out of here!" De Goulet shouts as he turns and draws his sword to fight.

The girls turn and run as the soldiers advance on the knights. Jay turns to see herself and Rowan ride away on the horse like they did just a few hours ago. She also sees her father and Pete escape.

Rowan turns just in time to see De Goulet fall to his knees. She sees three soldiers holding their swords inches from his throat. She screams in horror as Jay gently slaps her upper arm.

"Come on, Rowan," Jay says sadly. "We've gotta get out of here. We have to go now."

The two start running again. Their adrenaline allows them to run faster and longer. They are nearly to the time machine when they stop to catch their breath.

"It didn't work, Jay," Rowan says as she starts crying uncontrollably.

"I'm sorry, Rowan," Jay says with urgency in her voice. "We'll figure something out, but we've got to get out of here now."

"And go where," Rowan shouts. "I don't have anywhere to go."

"You have me, Rowan," Jay sympathetically tells her. "And together we're going to figure out how to fix this. We're gonna put everything right again but you need to be strong, and we need to get back to our time."

"I know," Rowan agrees. "I know you're right." She stops crying and straightens up, taking a deep breath.

"I'm alright," Rowan says after a long moment. "Let's do this. I wanna be me again." The two start walking at a quick pace and get back to the time machine in fifteen minutes.

They enter the container and Rowan secures the door as Jay activates the computer. The system starts its light show and a few minutes later Rowan opens the door.

The girls leave the abandoned building and for the next three hours quietly make their way back to Jay's house. They go in to find Jay's parents sitting at the table.

"Are you two okay?" Jay's mom asks. "You both look like you've been in a fight."

"We were in a fight," Jay tells them. "And we're still fighting."

"Fighting who?" Mom asks sarcastically.

"We're fighting for Rowan's identity," Jay tells her parents.

"When dad came back from his time machine experiment without Pete, Rowan and I went back in time to save him."

"When we came back we found out my ancestor was captured and I was never born," Rowan takes over. We went back to save him but it didn't work. He was captured by King Phillip's troops again."

"And so was Pete," Jay tells them. "I saw him get captured."

"And that's why we don't know you?" Mom asks her.

"Yes," Rowan replies. "Jay has been my best friend since kindergarten. I've spent half my life with the three of you. The two of you are like my second parents. You can't imagine how much this sucks."

"You're right, dear," Mom says. "I'm sorry but you're right, I can't imagine what you're going through."

"But I can," Dad says. "I know you're dealing with a lot, but we'll find a way to correct this problem."

"How, Dad?" Jay asks nearly in tears herself. "How can we fix this?"

"Well, I know when you were there the first time," Dad begins. "When did you go back the second time?"

"We were at the stables when we met you outside of the cathedral," Jay tells her parents.

"You were there when we met?" Asks dad with an odd look and strange tone.

"Let me get this straight," Mom interjects. "The two of you went back in time to see the two of you back in time meeting your father and Pete?" She catches her breath when she finishes.

"Yes," All three say simultaneously. They look at each other and laugh. Mom sits there silently with a bewildered look on her face.

"I don't get it," Mom says blankly.

"It's alright, my love," Dad says. "I got this." Dad glances at Jay and Rowan. "We got this."

"What are we going to do?" Jay asks.

"We're gonna go to the time machine," Dad says. "We'll make a plan along the way." The three get up and give mom kisses as they head toward the door.

Dad opens the door to see a police officer with his hand raised in a fist ready to knock.

"Hello," Dad says with a smile. "What can I do for you?"

"I've come to take you in," the officer says. "My captain wants to talk to you about Pete."

"What? Now?"

"Now," the officer replies, grabbing dad's arm forcefully.

Jay and Rowan look shocked while Mom looks at them with confusion. Dad turns to Jay and Rowan and tosses his car keys to Jay.

"It's up to you, Jay," Dad says with a smile. "You and Rowan."

"We'll figure it out Dad," Jay answers back.

CHAPTER 5

The girls are sitting in the car. Both are quietly thinking about the situation at hand. Jay is driving to the building that houses the time machine.

The car pulls behind the building and Jay shuts the engine off. The two sit in the dark quietly thinking.

"I got it," Jay shouts with enthusiasm. "We're gonna go back!"

"We can't go back," Rowan says. "We were there twice. A third set of us and somebody may see us and then we have the shoelace. Remember the shoelace?"

"Yes I do," Jay responds. "But we're not going back to 1307." She jumps out of the car and runs toward the broken window.

"Not 1307?" Rowan asks confused. "Then when are we going?"

Jay climbs through the window without answering with Rowan following closely.

They enter the container and, as before, Rowan secures the door as Jay boots up the computer. She begins keying in commands as Rowan sits beside her.

"What are you doing?" Rowan asks nearly shouting. "What year are we going to?"

"Irregardless of who used it, this is the same time machine," Jay begins. "The computer has data from every trip this machine has made."

"So," Rowan asks. "What can that do for us?"

"We're gonna go back to just before Dad and Pete take their first trip back."

"And?"

"And we'll stop them from leaving," Jay continues as she activates the time machine. "They won't go back in time. Pete won't get captured. We'll never have to go back."

"And Mozart De Goulet will never get captured and I'll get to be born," Rowan finishes.

"Exactly!" Jay says excitingly. "We're here." The two head for the door and step out into the present.

"What are the two of you doing in there?" Jay's dad asks angrily when the girls exit the container. "How did you get in there?"

"We used the machine to come back here to tell you that it works," Jay tells them.

"What are you talking about, Jay?" Dad asks. "What is she talking about, Rowan?"

"You… you know who I am?"

"Of course I do," Dad answers. "You practically grew up at our house." Rowan smiles widely and gives Jay's dad a long, tight hug. Jay joins in.

"Pete, get the time machine ready."

"What?" Jay sounds shocked. "You can't. You don't know what's gonna happen."

"Please don't go," Rowan adds. "There will be terrible consequences. Don't go." Both girls start crying.

"What is wrong with you two?" Dad asks.

"Dad, you and Pete already proved this works," Jay tells him. "You ended up in 1307. Pete was captured by King Phillip's soldiers when the Knights Templar were arrested."

"We went back to help you and my ancestor was captured because of us and I was never born," Rowan continues. "We went back again and my ancestor and Pete were captured again."

"So we came back here to stop you from going in the first place," Jay picks up the story again. "If you don't go when we get back to our present everything will be back to normal."

"Did you bring any proof of your trip, sweetie?" Dad asks with a lot of skepticism.

"No," Jay tells them. "We were to busy trying to help the two of you."

"Actually," Rowan chimes in as she takes out her cellphone. "I took some photos while we were there."

She activates her phone and taps her photo storage app. A series of photos appear on the screen. She shows them to Jay's dad and Pete.

"This is my ancestor, Mozart De Goulet, a Knights Templar." She moves to the next few photos. "This is the chapel in Metz, France, a stronghold of the Knights Templar.

"We were really there," Pete half asks, half tells.

"Yes, we were, and it was a disaster," Jay continues. "And it was worse for us on the second trip. Now we're here and as long as you don't go time will be repaired."

"Can I see your phone, Rowan?" Jay's dad politely asks the teen.

"Sure," She answers as she hands it to him. He takes her phone and scrolls through the photos that Rowan took in the past.

He and Pete examine each of the photos carefully. They look at the digital information as well as every detail of every image.

Pete activates the onboard computer and the two men go on the internet to research the authenticity of each picture.

After nearly fifteen minutes the men log off of the computer and return their attention to the girls.

"Can I download these photos to my computer?" Jay's dad asks Rowan.

"Sure," Rowan replies. "As long as you don't delete them."

"No problem," Jay's dad reassures her. "I'm only going to copy them to my hard drive."

"Okay, then," Rowan says with a smile. He plugs her cellphone into the computer and copies the photos to the hard drive.

It takes about a minute for the photos to download. Jay's dad unplugs Rowan's phone and gives it back to her.

Pete puts the photos on the monitor and starts to examine them even closer than before. He magnifies each image one at a time and searches the full picture.

"Well, Pete," Jay's dad asks. "Are the pictures real?"

"These pictures are amazing," Pete tells them. "Utterly remarkable. We were truly there. I wish I could remember it."

"Actually, we haven't gone yet," Jay's dad says. "And we won't be going any time soon."

What do you mean?" Pete asks in disbelief.

"I don't want to lose you in 1307," Jay's dad tells Pete. "We'll do more studying and find a safer time to visit."

"Look, you girls have been there," Pete begins. "You know what went wrong. If you came with us, we would only stay until the generators recharged. We would avoid all contact but we can take a few photos of our own and bring back a few samples."

"What do you think, Rowan?" Jay asks her best friend. "Could you deal with it if we all went together?"

"Yes, I believe I could," Rowan says with confidence. "As long as we avoid everyone."

"Absolutely," Jay's dad replies.

"Oh yes," Pete reiterates. "I don't want to get trapped in the past."

Jay's dad sits down and activates the initiation program and the coils glow and the air sparkles. Rowan opens the door when the sequence ends.

The four walk quietly through the forest to the edge of the city of Metz. Pete takes out his camera and starts photographing the city and cathedral.

The four see a man on horseback ride out of the forest a thousand yards away.

"That is my ancestor, Mozart de Goulet," Rowan tells Jay's dad and Pete.

Pete aims his camera at the unsuspecting knight and snaps a series of photos.

"Are you ready to go back," Rowan asks. "We are risking a lot. I think we need to go."

"You're right, Rowan," Jay says. "Let's go, dad, Pete. We need to leave before something bad happens."

"I got what I need," Pete tells them.

"Well, then," Jay's dad says. "Let's get out of here."

The four make their way back in the direction they came. They get to a clearing about a quarter of a mile from the time machine when a noise catches their attention.

"Halt!" A loud voice commands. "In the name of King Phillip of France, Stop!"

The four look to the right to see a soldier on horseback with his sword drawn and lifted above his head. He glares at the four pedestrians and repeats his previous command.

Jay and Rowan look up at Jay's dad and Pete. The two men look at each other then at the girls.

"Ready?" Jay's dad asks the group and they nod in agreement. Without another word and any other warning, the four turn and start running at full speed toward the time machine.

"Halt!" The soldier repeats as he commands his horse to charge. The horse races toward the quartet as they run for the opening in the forest.

The four make it to the forest before the horse and rider and disappear into the darkness. The soldier stops his horse several yards along the path when the tree growth blocks out all of the moonlight.

The quartet stop running when they get to the cargo container.

"Is everyone okay?" Jay's dad asks in between breaths.

The three acknowledge as Rowan opens the container.

"That was close," Jay says.

"Too close," Rowan adds. "Let's get out of here." They all agree and get inside the container. Rowan secures the door. The light show ends and the four find themselves home.

"Now we've got to get back to our time," Jay tells her dad and Pete. "Now that we've been there, and nobody was captured, when we get back everything should be fixed."

The group spends the next two hours reviewing the photographs that Pete took in the past. The computer interrupts their viewing when the generators are charged.

Jay and Rowan go back into the time machine and activate the unit. The two exit the time machine and secure it before leaving the building.

They get outside and find Jay's dad's car still parked in the back. They get in the car and head straight to Jay's house.

"Where have you two been?" Jay's mom asks angrily. "I've been worried sick." She turns her attention to Rowan. "Your mother has called here three times."

A huge smile spreads across Rowan's face when she hears the news. She looks at Jay whose smile is just as big.

"I think I'm gonna go home," Rowan tells Jay, who simply nods in agreement. Rowan leaves her best friend's house without another word.

A few minutes after Rowan leaves, Jay's dad comes in the door. Upon seeing each other they just smile widely while Jay's mom looks on confused.

The two explain what happened to Jay's mom who just looks at them blankly, not understanding what they're talking about.

Jay's cellphone rings. She looks at the screen and, seeing it is Rowan, she answers it.

"Hey, Rowan, what's up?" Jay asks her.

"I wanted to let you know, Jay," Rowan's voice sounds happy, "I got home and everything is the same as it was when you woke me up this morning."

"That's great news, Rowan. I'll see you tomorrow."

JAY AND ROWAN
IN TIME

COLORING BOOK

JAY

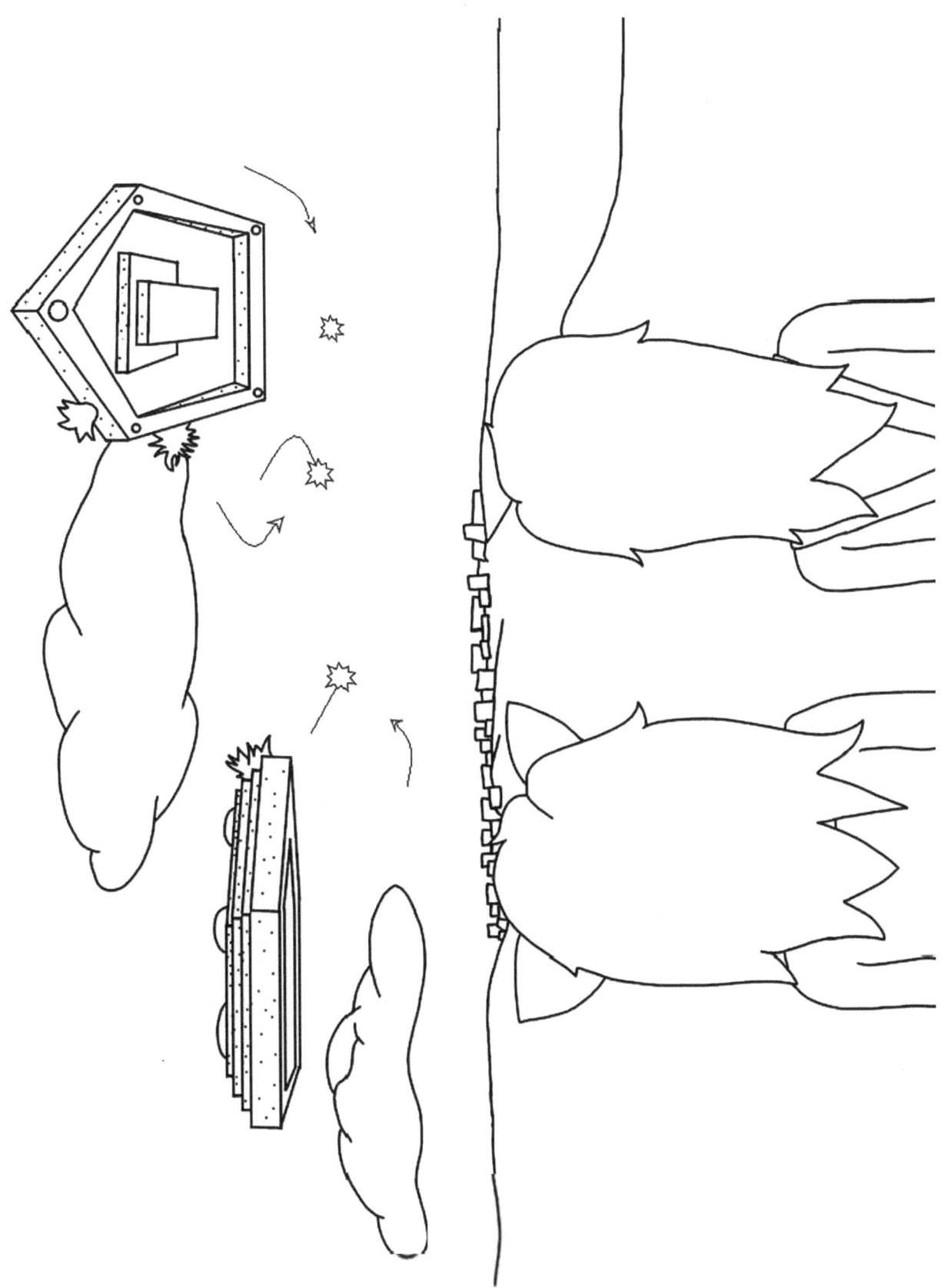

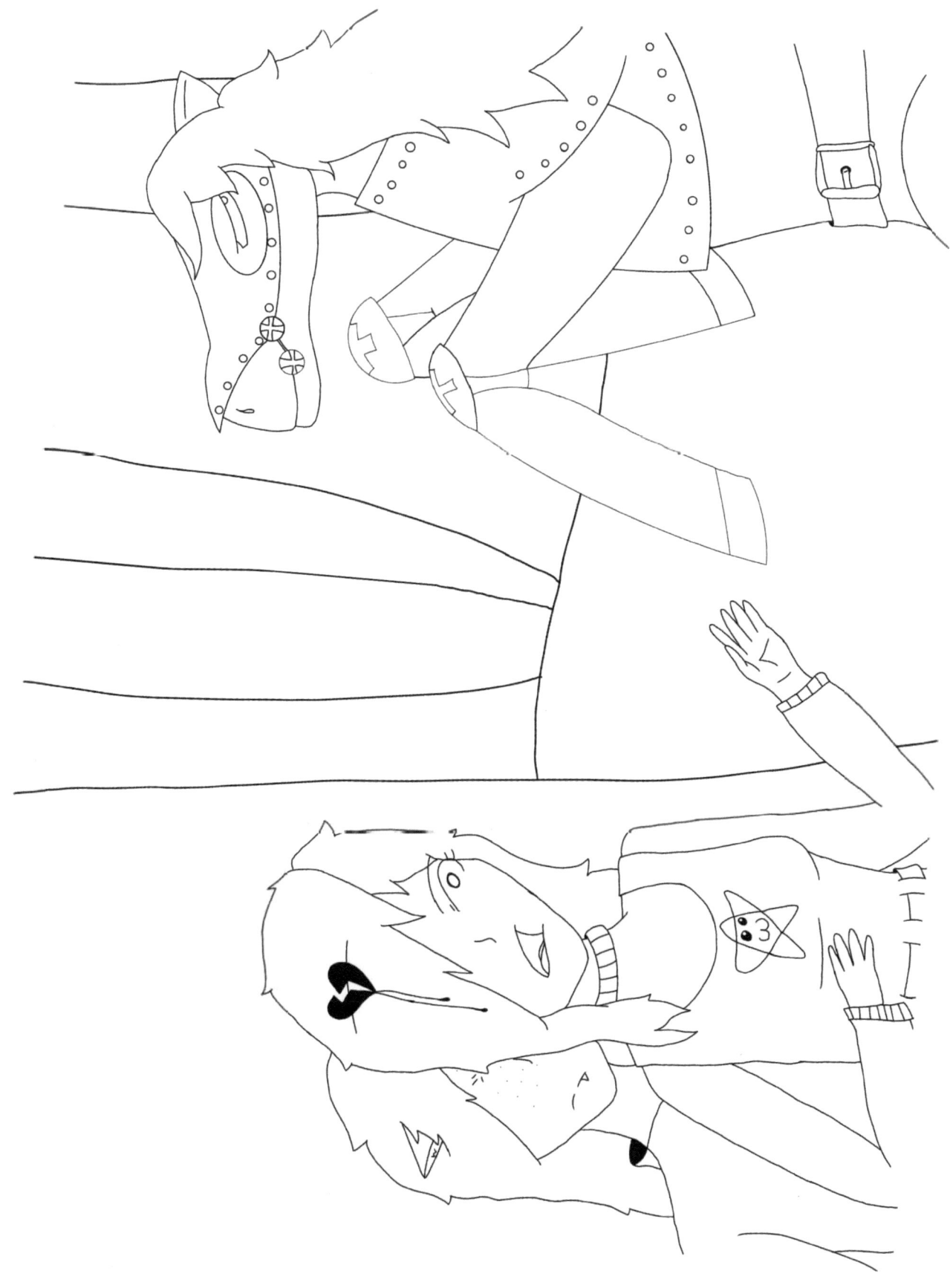

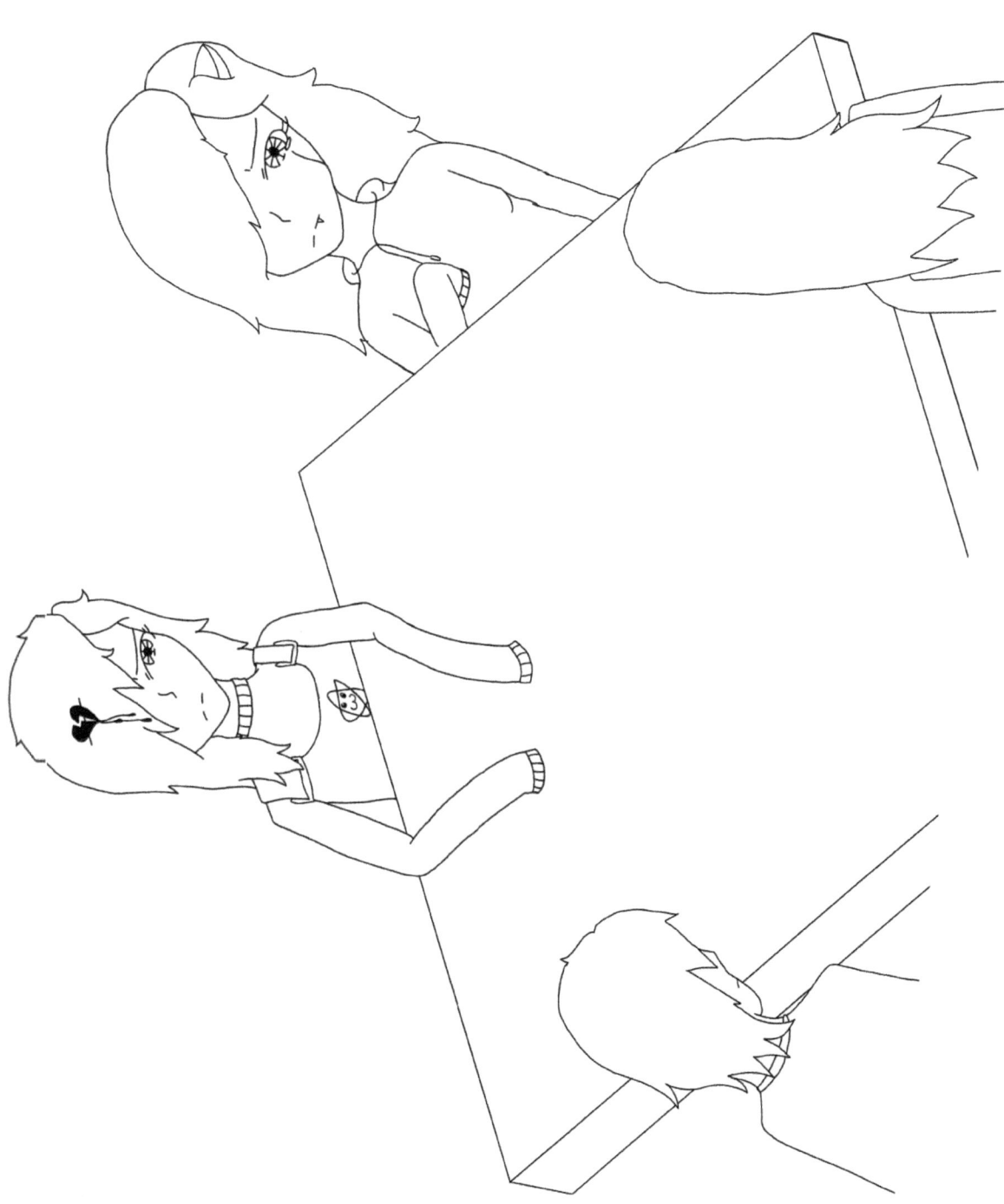

ABOUT THE AUTHOR

   The Author is **R.N. Chevalier**, who also wrote a sci-fi, action-adventure trilogy consisting of *Are We the Klingons*, *Advances Of The Ancients* and *Full Circle*, after having been diagnosed with ALS in 2012. He also coauthored, along with his wife, Donna the *Rhode Island Civil War Monuments-A Pictorial Guide*. The pair also host the website ForzakEmpire.com.

   The Illustrator is **"Jay" Chevalier**. She is the 18 year old daughter of the author who is currently a high school senior attending CCRI as a college freshman in the Running Start program. Jay not only is her nickname but also who the character, Jay, is molded after. She started using sketching as a focusing tool and was diagnosed with Severe Depression and High Anxiety a short time later. She created a host of characters including all the ones in this book, in her unique style. She is an animal lover who is also an aficionado of the lolita fashion.

www.ingramcontent.com/pod-product-compliance
Lightning Source LLC
Chambersburg PA
CBHW041535240626
47164CB00002B/26